ISBN 978-1-334-41530-2
PIBN 10752985

This book is a reproduction of an important historical work. Forgotten Books uses
state-of-the-art technology to digitally reconstruct the work, preserving the original format
whilst repairing imperfections present in the aged copy. In rare cases, an imperfection in
the original, such as a blemish or missing page, may be replicated in our edition. We do,
however, repair the vast majority of imperfections successfully; any imperfections that
remain are intentionally left to preserve the state of such historical works.

1 MONTH OF FREE READING

at
www.ForgottenBooks.com

By purchasing this book you are eligible for one month membership to ForgottenBooks.com, giving you unlimited access to our entire collection of over 700,000 titles via our web site and mobile apps.

To claim your free month visit:
www.forgottenbooks.com/free752985

English
Français
Deutsche
Italiano
Español
Português

www.forgottenbooks.com

Mythology Photography **Fiction**
Fishing Christianity **Art** Cooking
Essays Buddhism Freemasonry
Medicine **Biology** Music **Ancient
Egypt** Evolution Carpentry Physics
Dance Geology **Mathematics** Fitness
Shakespeare **Folklore** Yoga Marketing
Confidence Immortality Biographies
Poetry **Psychology** Witchcraft
Electronics Chemistry History **Law**
Accounting **Philosophy** Anthropology
Alchemy Drama Quantum Mechanics
Atheism Sexual Health **Ancient History**
Entrepreneurship Languages Sport
Paleontology Needlework Islam
Metaphysics Investment Archaeology
Parenting Statistics Criminology
Motivational

French's International Copyrighted (in England, her Colonies, and the United States) Edition of the Works of the Best Authors

35

No. 260.

1

ROOM 83

A Farce in One Act

BY

MORTON WEIL

Elaborated by

MARION SHORT

PRICE 25 CENTS

NEW YORK
SAMUEL FRENCH
PUBLISHER
28-30 WEST 38TH STREET

LONDON
SAMUEL FRENCH, LTD.
26 SOUTHAMPTON STREET
STRAND

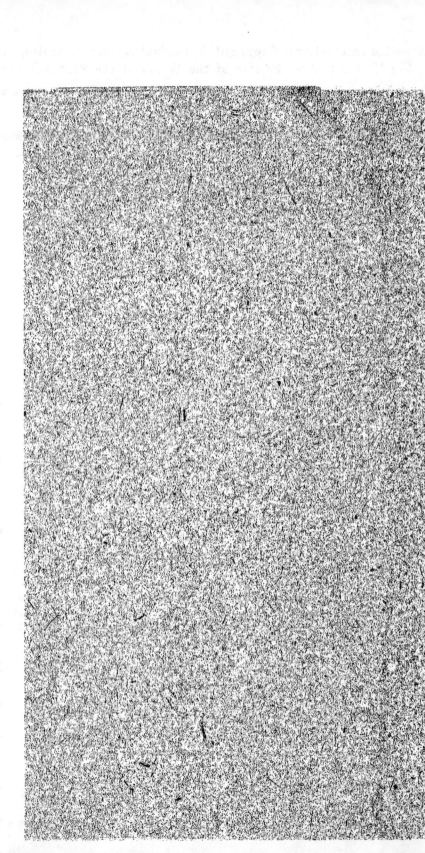

ROOM 83

A Farce in One Act

BY

MORTON WEIL

Elaborated by

MARION SHORT

COPYRIGHT, 1913, BY SAMUEL FRENCH

NEW YORK
SAMUEL FRENCH
PUBLISHER
28–30 WEST 38TH STREET

LONDON
SAMUEL FRENCH, LTD.
26 SOUTHAMPTON STREET
STRAND

ROOM 83.

SCENE:—*Nicely furnished room in Palace Hotel, New York. Tea-table* C. *with service, and chairs at either side. Arm-chair* R. *On wall* R. *(or above mantel-piece) a mirror. Sofa* L.

TIME.—*Now.*

CHARACTERS.

HARRY WASHINGTON, of Mount Vernon, N. Y.
ELSIE WASHINGTON, *his wife.*
CHARLES CRANE, *of Craneville, N. J.*
MARIE CRANE, *his wife.*

ROOM 83.

DISCOVERED. HARRY WASHINGTON *at* R. *of table, completely hidden behind the open newspaper in his hands.*

ELSIE. (*enters door* C. *and comes down to other side of table where* HARRY *is sitting absorbed in newspaper*) Harry!

HARRY. (*unheedingly*) Cotton going down.

ELSIE. (*irritated, and gesturing with a letter she holds in her hand*) I don't care where cotton goes, or when—unless I happen to have the ear-ache. What do you think?

HARRY. I think the jury will acquit her, even if everyone knows she did shoot him. (*continues to reads*)

ELSIE. Oh, bother your old newspaper! I was talking about this letter that just came.

HARRY. (*waving her off with one hand as he brings paper closer to his eyes*) Only four more pages to read!

ELSIE. (*walks away in a temper*) Talk about the drink habit, or the gambling habit—there's nothing so maddening to a woman as to have her husband acquire the newspaper habit. Read, read, read if the world comes to an end!

HARRY. Suppose it does come to an end? Wouldn't you wish your husband to read about it in advance? Don't you wish him to be well informed?

ELSIE. Well informed? Yes. That's why I am

3

trying to inform you now what's in this letter from
Cousin Mollie!

HARRY. (*springs up excitedly, flinging paper to
one side*) Cousin Mollie!

ELSIE. (*sarcastically*) But you won't let me—
you're too wrapped up in cotton and whether she shot
him or not, and baseball, and—and—(*gestures dis-
gustedly*) fudge!

HARRY. (*enthusiastically*) Cousin Mollie! Our
one rich relative—our star of hope! (*in injured
tone*) Why didn't you say so at once?

ELSIE. (*thinking she has the upper hand, holds
letter behind her back*) Oh, you've four more pages
to read! After that—I'll let you know.

HARRY. All right. (*starts to pick up paper.*)

ELSIE. (*snatches it away*) Don't you dare read
in the midst of my conversation!

HARRY. Well, what does she say?

ELSIE. That she's coming on here from the West
to visit us, and bring her brother Tom.

HARRY. Great Caesar's immortal shade—how
sudden!

ELSIE. (*ruefully*) Talk about cotton going down.
If they once visit us—it means a fortune going up.

HARRY. Why do you say that?

ELSIE. The only reason why Mollie willed me her
money is because she has never seen me.

HARRY. Come now—you may not be a beauty,
but you're not so bad as all that!

ELSIE. What I mean is—she has a dreadful dispo-
sition and can't get along with anyone. She's quar-
reled with every relative on earth that she HAS seen
and cut them out of her will one by one, and now it
has come my turn!

HARRY. But she shan't cut you off. I—I've
thought of that money so long that I've become fond
of it. It would actually hurt my feelings to lose it
now. Make up your mind to try your level best to

make her like you so she'll keep the will intact. She's bound to approve of me naturally—all women do!

(Thumbs in armholes.)

ELSIE. Until they marry you!

HARRY. Now, you don't mean that—I know you don't!

ELSIE. It makes me angry to see you so eager about that money—and not one word to say about— about half an hour from now.

HARRY. Half an hour from now? *(puzzled)* What's the answer?

ELSIE. *(with a hint of tears)* In half an hour we'll have been married just two years. But of course that's nothing to you, and Cousin Mollie's money is everything!

HARRY. In half an hour, my precious, I'll beg for an anniversary kiss! Compared to the sweetness of that—believe me the money will be nothing—nothing —Why in thunder doesn't she come if she's coming and not be wasting time on letters?

ELSIE. That's all the good it will do us when she DOES come. My trying to be pleasant and your natural attractiveness will fail to work. The truth is—Cousin Mollie and Tom are both as crazy as March hares.

HARRY. Not actually crazy?

ELSIE. Called by courtesy eccentric because they have money. If poor like us, they'd be carted off to a county asylum in a jiffy. She's a fiend—and I know she'll turn against me and yearn to murder me with a hat-pin at sight!

HARRY. What does the letter say?

ELSIE. *(reads)* "Dear Cousin Elsie:—Brother Tommie and I are tired of the West. We are a trifle more than up-to-date, and everyone says we're crazy. Between you and me everyone in this state is crazy except ourselves. We're coming to visit you at that hotel in New York, apartment 83, where you stay one month in each year. As we start at once we may reach you before this letter does. In that case you may read us first. Or, we and the letter may arrive hand in hand. Anyhow I remain your affectionate COUSIN MOLLIE."

HARRY. (*who has been thinking hard during reading of letter*) I have the situation managed perfectly already!

ELSIE. So have I?

HARRY. What's your idea?

ELSIE. To leave the hotel immediately with word that we've sailed for Europe. My only chance of keeping in her good graces and from being cut off in her will—is to stay carefully out of her sight. I'll 'phone for a taxi right now. (*starts for door*)

HARRY. (*following and detaining her*) Won't you listen to little hubby for a minute?

ELSIE. In a minute they may be here!

HARRY. Let them come! Keep your head and follow my directions—and we'll emerge on top of the haystack!

ELSIE. Anyhow you know what a timid thing I am! Do you think I want a couple of lunatics rambling around our rooms? No!! Fortune or no fortune!

HARRY. Do you think I want to offend her by running away and lose thereby a nice big barrel of money? No! Lunatic or no lunatic! Believe me! Not on your tin-type! We've got to stay and jolly Mollie!

ELSIE. (*with exaggerated waves of impatience in her voice.*) Stay and jolly Mollie?

HARRY. You needn't sing it! It's not a song— it's a suggestion! Now, listen, lovey. (*puts arm about her and brings her down stage*) The way to get along with crazy people is to humor them. Do everything that they do—no matter what it is! It flatters their vanity. Why, it's a cinch and simple as a, b, c! Anyhow, she may not be crazy at all!

ELSIE. She made me her sole heir—doesn't that prove it?

HARRY. Proves it's a pleasant kind of derange- ment. Wish some of my relatives would catch it!

ELSIE. Oh, but I'm so afraid of craziness! (*as if aggrieved*) Why did she pick me out for her sole heir anyhow?

HARRY. Heavens, you lament it? Bear up, Elsie, I'll help you to spend the barrel when it bursts. As a splender you will find I have few equals and no superiors. As to why she selected you—you're prob- ably the only relative who hasn't tried to insert her into a straight jacket or hit her over the head with a chair when she became violent.

ELSIE. Violent? (*shudders with fear*) Oh! I see her coming at me with a hat-pin as in a vision! I won't stay here—I won't meet them!

HARRY. (*angry*) Won't?

ELSIE. Won't!

HARRY. Then you're just as crazy as they are!

ELSIE. I suppose you'd like me to just stand still and let them murder me! What good will their money do me after they've punctured me with a hat- pin and I'm dead? I'll 'phone for that taxi. Europe for mine!

HARRY. (*appealing with great sentiment*) Now, listen to reason, lovey dovey honey-bunch! (*follows her as she exits door up* R.) Now, Pettie winkles just a word—(*exits after her up* R.)

(*Door* C. *opens suddenly and* CHARLES CRANE *with his wife enter. They are both in street clothes.*)

CHARLES. (*on entering*) This is room 88! (*briskly*) We were to walk right in and make our- selves at home, the lawyer said. (*looks about ap-*

preciatively as he lays off hat and puts cane in cor-
ner) Pretty nice quarters Uncle Billy occupied all
right all right!

MARIE. (*making wide-spreading gesture*) Heavens it's like a dream!

CHARLES. Gold coins and greenbacks coming to
life!

MARIE. To think that in a few days you'll be
worth half a million dollars!

CHARLES. A full million, if Cousin Julia and her
mother hadn't come along and jollied him into turn-
ing half of it over to them!

MARIE. I wonder how she did it! Is she pretty?

CHARLES. Never saw either her or her brother.
But they'll arrive any minute now to talk things
over. The money is tied up for five long years unless we mutually agree to sign a paper that turns it
over to us at once.

MARIE. Well, you must sign it instanter!

CHARLES. Of course. But will she? There's the
rub!

MARIE. Wouldn't it be horrible if she should in-
sist on keeping it tied up—just when I need six new
hats and eleven new gowns so badly that I'm dis-
graced without them.

CHARLES. I feel certain I could argue her into
my way of thinking and get immediate possession of
the cash if it weren't for—(*hesitates*)

MARIE. For what?

CHARLES. (*hesitatingly*) I don't like to own
up to it as they're my cousins—but they're both sup-
posed to be off a little in the upper story—dippy, in
fact. She may conclude she'd rather have the money
tied up for five years and——

MARIE. And of course you can't argue with craziness.

CHARLES. But you can manage if you know how.
I shall jolly her, and fall apparently into her way
of thinking. That's the experiment I've decided on,

so if you see me walk up to her and chuck her under the chin——

MARIE. (*imperiously*) No chucking and no chin!

CHARLES. Not even for half a million?

MARIE. Not even for half a squillion! You know my one failing, do you not?

CHARLES. (*ruefully, showing fear of her*) Jeallousy—yes, I know! But just for the time being—and when it would mean all the hats and gowns you want inside of a week——

MARIE. (*passionately*) I believe you've always been in love with her!

CHARLES. I've never even seen her. I told you.

MARIE. (*suspiciously*). But, you may have loved her from a distance!

CHARLES. (*wearily*) Keep it up, Mrs. Othello!

MARIE. No chin and no chucks—I warn you!

CHARLES. (*obediently*) I cut out the chin and chuck the chucks.

MARIE. (*satisfied*) Very well.

CHARLES. But, for heaven's sake don't be watching every move I make, or you'll get my nerves on edge. (*looks at watch*) I wish they'd come.

MARIE. (*gazing in mirror*) There, my hat has worked crooked again! I lost my hat-pin on the way here, and it simply will not stay oon straight.

CHARLES. (*matter of fact manner*). Why not take it off?

MARIE. And have you compare me unfavorably with your cousin Julia whom you have just been telling me is beautiful? I guess not. The hat happens to be becoming and on it stays.

CHARLES. But, Marie, I never said she was beautiful. How could I when I've not seen her?

MARIE. (*strolling about*) I thought you said there'd be a picture of your Uncle Billy hanging over the mantel-piece. You're certain this is his room?

CHARLES. Of course—suite 88. Wasn't it on the door?

MARIE. I didn't look. I was watching the chamber-maid watch you, and you——

CHARLES. I never even looked at her. She's too cross-eyed to make a hit with me.

MARIE. How did you know she was cross-eyed?

CHARLES. A clever guess, my darling. Now, you're not going to show jealousy of Cousin Julia, are you?

MARIE. N-no. But all the same I shall keep on my bcoming hat even if it is uncomfortable without a hat-pin. She shan't have me at a disadvantage.

CHARLES. Let me straighten it for you, little pudding-pie! (*straightens her hat*)

(*Enter door* R. HARRY *and* ELSIE *unobserved.*)

HARRY. (*in low tone to* ELSIE, *nodding head toward other couple*) I told you I heard voices!

ELSIE. My crazy cousins of course! Oh, I'm so afraid. (*clings to his arm*)

HARRY. (*valiant and important*) Follow my lead—follow my lead—watch me jolly them. (*suddenly and loudly*) Hello! Glad to see you!

MARIE. (*to* CHARLES) Your lunatics! When did they get here?

CHARLES. (*to* HARRY) Hello yourself. Who are you?

MARIE. (*warningly as he goes toward them*) No chucks!

HARRY. (*to* ELSIE) Speak up—be pleasant!

ELSIE. (*plainly frightened*) W-we are your cousins, and you are w-welcome!

MARIE. (*as he is about to shake hands with* ELSIE) No chin!

(ELSIE, *frightened, draws back without giving* CHARLES *her hand.*)

HARRY. (*aside to* ELSIE) 'Smile—smile—don't let 'em think they scare you! (*gives hand to* CHARLES) We know—the will—the will—and all that! (*nods and winks extravagantly; overdoes being pleasant altogether while* MARIE *and* HARRY *look at him and exchange significant glances*)

MARIE. (*walks toward* ELSIE) How do you do, cousin?

ELSIE. (*frightened*) W-wery vell, I thank you.

MARIE. You don't happen to have a hat-pin handy, do you?

ELSIE. No, no, no! (*runs and get behind* HARRY) She wants a hat-pin. What did I tell you.

MARIE. (*to* CHARLES) Poor little thing! No sense at all. Almost blithering! I'll try to ignore it.

CHARLES. That's right.

MARIE. (*approaching* ELSIE *and* HARRY *again*) I just thought if I could get hold of a hat-pin——

HARRY. (*shows a bit of fright himself as* ELSIE *clings to him, then braces up*) Dear lady, we have no hat-pins, nor daggers, nor other sharp instruments. (*laughs hollowly and conciliatingly*) We—we never play with them in our yard—so to speak!

MARIE. (*pleasantly*) Well, I don't wish to trouble you, of course—but I thought if I could just give one little stab——

ELSIE. Oh! (*pulls* RARRY *to one side of room and peers from behind him wild-eyed at other couple*)

MARIE. (*returns to* CHARLES) Isn't she the craziest ever? Acts afraid of something!

CHARLES. I'll calm her.

MARIE. All right, but no chins, remember!

CHARLES. (*to* ELSIE) The reason she asked for a hat-pin is——

ELSIE. (*falls on knees before him*) I know! I saw it in a vision! Oh, but you won't let her puncture me, you won't!

CHARLES. Don't be frightened! Why—(*leans down*)

MARIE. (*shrieks warningly*) No chucks!

CHARLES. (*backs off a bit, disconcerted by wife's interruption*) Nothing shall harm you—I give my word!

MARIE. Isn't she pathetic—and so young?

HARRY. Be seated everybody. (*all take seats*) I hope your stay in town will be very pleasant.

MARIE. (*exaggerated politeness*) It's been very pleasant so far!

ELSIE. (*aside*) Oh! (*hand to head indicating mental distress*)

HARRY. Of course, as you already know—my name is Washington.

MARIE. (*half whisper to* CHARLES) It isn't, is it?

CHARLES. No, but I'll humor him if he thinks it is. (*rises*) Being George Washington, you may perhaps like to know who I am. Napolecn Bonaparte, at your service.. (*frowns, draws down chin, folds arm and stands in characteristic Napoleonic attitude*)

HARRY. (*aside to* ELSIE) Crazy as the girl—and worse. (*pleasantly, to* CHARLES) Sure thing, Nappy, old boy! Knew you were from St. Helena the minute I saw you. You have that—that—banished expression, you know! This is Martha Washington—my wife! (*drags the reluctant* ELSIE *forward*).

CHARLES. (*brings* MARIE *forward*) And this is the Empress Josephine! (*aside to* MARIE) Humor them—humor them—it means that money now remember!

HARRY. (*aside to* ELSIE) Do as they do—imitate them—or she'll cut you out of her will.

MARIE. (*comes forward with ceremonial effusiveness*) Mrs. General Washington—I'm delighted. (*makes very deep courtesy*)

ELSIE. Charmed, Empress Josephine! (*makes deep bow and nervously drops her fan*)

CHARLES. Permit me! (*makes such a sudden dive for fan that he falls over. The women keep on bowing and* MARIE'S *hat falls to the floor*)

HARRY. Permit me! (*dives for hat and falls in same way* CHARLES *has done. As he rises and restores hat,* ELSIE *drops fan again while bowing and* CHARLES *falls as before and gives it back to her. Then* MARIE'S *hat falls off and* HARRY *falls again in giving it back to her. Business kept up as long as it goes. Then* MARIE *bows so profoundly that she falls in a sitting posture and* ELSIE *does likewise.* CHARLES *and* HARRY *fall as before in restoring to them their respective property. All, disheveled, remain sitting on floor*)

MARIE. (*almost savagely, as she slams hat wrong side to on her head*) I demand a hat-pin!

ELSIE. (*shrieks her words hysterically*) What do you want of it?

MARIE. To put through my hat—what do you suppose?

ELSIE. Why didn't you say so in the first place?

(*All scramble to their feet.*)

MARIE. (*walks to one side with* CHARLES) Why don't you ask her whether she's going to sign, and have it over with?

CHARLES. Waiting to have her take the lead, that's all, and then falling in (*rubs knee rather ruefully*) and falling down. I've got to get my breath. (*sits in chair* L. MARIE *fans him with his hat*)

HARRY. (*at* R. *with* ELSIE, *speaks as if half out of breath*) You mustn't show temper, sugar-lump, otherwise we're entertaining them very nicely I think. Phew! I haven't had so much exercise since I was quarter-back at college! But the money's worth it!

ELSIE. (*aggrieved*) Oh, that old money of hers is everything you think of!

HARRY. What else is there to remember just now, my love?

ELSIE. (*her voice trembling*) Our anniversary kiss! I told you you'd forget it.

HARRY. But, I didn't, duckie. (*fans himself with handkerchief*) Can't you see that I'm panting with anticipation? (*she walks further to* R., *pouting. He takes long step toward her on each count*) One, two, three, (*kisses her loudly*) there! (*turns to* CHARLES) You'll have too excuse publicity!

CHARLES. (*gets to his feet, smiling fatuously*) Why, certainly! (*speaks aside to* MARIE) I'm obliged to imitate him, my love.

MARIE. Very well! (*walks smilingly further to* L. *and stands with cheek raised waiting for the caress.* CHARLES *prepares to walk toward* ELSIE *instead*)

CHARLES. (*takes strides similar to* HARRY'S) One, two, three—(*bends to kiss* ELSIE. *She slaps him as she says word to complete his sentence*)

ELSIE. There! (CHARLES *puts hand to cheek and makes wry face*) How dare you?

MARIE. (*pulls* CHARLES *back and faces* ELSIE *instead*) How dare you inveigle my husband into kissing you, you lobster-eyed, shrimp-nosed blue-fish?

(ELSIE *shrieks and runs to other side of room.*)

HARRY. (*to* CHARLES) You tried to kiss my wife, you pusillanimous pin-head. (*shakes fist at* Charles.

CHARLES. Stand back! You don't understand! (*takes a step toward him*)

HARRY. Wow! You stepped on my pet corn! (*takes foot in hand*)

CHARLES. You shouldn't keep such pets.

MARIE. (*pulls* CHARLES *away*) You're forgetting what we came for!

ELSIE. (*to* HARRY. We mustn't lose our tempers. You said we should imitate them, and——

HARRY. (*furious, still nursing foot*) Imitate them? That's what I said and I intend to keep my word. He roosted on my corn! (*calls to* CHARLES *as he hops about on one foot*) Come over here—I want to roost on yours! Wow!

MARIE. What is the creature wowing about?

ELSIE. (*losing her temper*) You shan't call my husband a "creature," in addition to walking on his feet! Oh, my courage has all come back to me! (*produces letter she read to* HARRY *at opening of act*) Here's your old letter telling me to expect you. I return it! Cut me out of your will—I don't care! Just so we're rid of you once for all!

MARIE. (*takes letter, looks at address on envelope*) But I never wrote this! Besides it is addressed to room 83, and this is room 88.

CHARLES. Certainly—room 88.

HARRY. Is, eh? (*hobbles and opens door*) There!

(*Large figure 83 visible on door.*)

MARIE. 83 sure enough! (*to* CHARLES) It is not your Uncle Billy's room at all and never was!

CHARLES. (*disgruntled*) Bad light in the hall— I couldn't see. (*apologetically bows to* HARRY *and* ELSIE) Wrong room! We are intruders. I beg the pardon of you both even if you ARE crazy.

HARRY. Crazy. It's YOU that is the lunatic, Napoleon Bonaparte!

CHARLES. No, YOU, Father of our Country, are the one with the wabbly headpiece. My name is Crane, plain Charles Crane of Craneville, N. J.

HARRY. And I am plain Harry Washington of Mount Vernon, New York.

CHARLES. (*testily*) Well, if you *aren't* crazy, you look it!

HARRY. Well, if you aren't—you ACT it. (*turns to* ELSIE, *his rage increasing*) I've had enough of this. Come on away from here instanter. (*starts toward door up* R.)

ELSIE. Come where?

HARRY. (*shouts at the top of his lungs*) To Europe. (*exits door up* R.)

CHARLES. (*also in a rage, turns to* MARIE) Follow me!

MARIE. Where? To room 88?

CHARLES. Room 88 be hanged. HOME! (*slams on his hat and exits door* C.)

MARIE. (*with calm condescension*) Aren't men foolish? I knew there was a mistake of some kind,

ELSIE. (*equally calm and lofty*) So did I—all along!

(*Men put heads in doors* R. *and* C. *simultaneously and roar at the women*)

COME ON!

CURTAIN.

9 781334 415302